MURDER OF
MUMBAI MURRAY

A Selena Sharma Mystery

By

C T Mitchell

Copyright

TABLE OF CONTENTS

CHAPTER 1

"Papa-ji, I would love to chat but I have got to finish a large order for an important client" Selena replied to her pressing father, her mobile phone cocked between her right ear and shoulder while she lovingly stirred a large pot of butter chicken, sampling it as she went. "I promise to call back during the week. Love you Papa-ji" as she tossed her phone across the benchtop sliding into the tile splash back with force.

Rousi Sharma checked in on his daughter regularly. She was his only child and he missed her very much, just like most father's do of their daughters who had moved out of home. Selena was a little further from India than Rousi liked.

Selena loved her Dad but his constant chat about her returning to India to run the family's rice business sometimes wore thin on Selena. She appreciated what her father had done for the family but she wanted to make her own way in the world.

She probably got her independent streak from her mother. Anita Sharma dutifully played the perfect wife but was not one to be bossed around; something Rousi struggled with at times. Now his only child had inherited her mother's deter-mined nature. But overall, Rousi was very proud of his Selena.

Cameron Stewart looked up from the verandah, momentarily putting his glass of Peter Lehmann Shiraz on the table to enquire "Daddy still wants you to go home to marry your rich boyfriend, eh?" delivered in a patronizing tone coupled with a cheeky smile. He knew he would get a bite.

"There is no boyfriend Detective!" adding some formality to the conversation "but I'm just not in the mood for one of papa-ji's lectures. I've got to get this order over to Mr. Barrington- Jones' home tonight before it gets too dark. He's feeding the construction crew tomorrow."

Cameron Stewart smiled and returned the red to his mouth to savor another drop while patting Hudson, his eight-year-old British bulldog, who sat attentively by his feet, busily licking his fingers and hoping he would earn his very own beef samosa soon.

Stewart broke off a small piece of crust and spicy meat and dropped it on the deck. Hudson hoovered it down in one gulp, licking his chops and fixing his blood shot eyes back onto Detective Stewart, hoping his best puppy dog face would weaken his master. But Stewart too loved Selena's fine delicacies and Hudson was left to once again salivate all over Selena's verandah.

"You don't think the samosas will be too spicy for Hudson, do you?"

"A bit of spice is good for everybody" Selena replied from the kitchen hoping to lock eyes with Cameron but alas he was fixated on his next bite, her comment washing over him without even stirring an emotional ripple. Selena secretly hoped that one day the penny would drop with Cameron Stewart.

Maybe Cameron was all consumed with the Indian custom of arranged marriages Selena pondered and that was holding his feelings back. She would do everything to dispel thoughts in Cameron.

"What do you make of Barrington-Jones?" Stewart asked. "This development he's about to start has got the whole town talking. He seems to be a bit of a wheeler dealer to me"

Stewart had a right to be concerned. Murray Barrington-Jones, known around town as 'Mumbai Murray', had brought a lot of investment into the area, particularly from India, but his methods were questionable. Originally, he operated as a business migration agent, resettling a number of Indian families into the region. The Kumar's were one of his original clients and soon after established Pottsville's first Indian restaurant.

But people selling dreams to foreigners wanting to relocate to the region and enjoy a better life, didn't seem to be lucrative enough for Murray. A few years back he became a property investment consultant and added home sales to his migration agency.

Rumors of dodgy selling practices soon emerged even down to the playing of Bollywood music in Murray's big black Mercedes Benz ML 350 while customers munched on Bhuja nuts as they were whisked from overpriced property to overpriced property.

But Barrington-Jones' charm resonated with his Indian customers who soon adorned him with the title Mumbai Murray, as Barrington-Jones was a mouthful for his mostly non-English speaking clientele.

"Maybe Mr. Stewart, but Pottsville has to thank him for investment here. I think Chadani Group is financially backing him on his golf course project; they are huge back in India." Deepak Chadani's son would be a great catch for most Indian women, except for the independent Selena.

"I'm guessing your father sells rice to them?" a tongue in cheek Stewart smirked.

"I doubt it but at least his daughter will be feeding their construction crew tomorrow, if I ever get these meals finished and delivered"

"I think I should go with you when you deliver the meals" a protective sounding Cameron Stewart piped up "or at least you should take Hudson with you. He would love a drive in your flash, red Mercedes sports car, especially after knocking down four of your finest samosas."

For a moment Selena had thought Detective Stewart was warming to her, but perhaps not. She sighed and looked at Hudson who was making a nice mess of her verandah.

"I'll be fine. I think the golf course will be great for Pottsville and the Country Club will bring in people from far and wide for Sunday lunch. I might finally meet 'Mr. Right' there" Selena smarted back hoping to twist cupid's arrow into Cameron Stewart's heart. Bu there again as the Aussies would say *it went straight through to the keeper.*

Selena shuffled out to her car, opened the passenger door, and signaled for Hudson to jump in. But Hudson's short stocky statue carrying an unhealthy 30 kg of weight required help from Selena to place him on the front seat.

Forty containers of butter chicken and rice were carefully placed in the Merc's boot protected in a polystyrene box ensuring they didn't slide around and stayed warm for Mumbai Murray. Driving away from the guesthouse Selena waved to Stewart advising him that she would drop Hudson off to his place on her way home.

Cameron Stewart watched as the red Mercedes puffed up the dust as Selena slipped further into the distance. He did worry about Selena but couldn't express himself. Secretly, she was the bright light that kept him in the area as the local detective, having knocked back promotion after promotion to move to a bigger region.

What if she did find 'Mr. Right' at Mumbai Murray's Oasis Country Club and Golf Course in the future? He knew he would be devastated but he couldn't bring himself to show his feeling.

Besides, Rousi Sharma would probably get his way and eventually Selena would return home to marry the son of a wealthy industrialist or commerce baron, her rightful place but a marriage without love; possibly.

Stewart sighed knowing his paltry salary as a police officer paled into insignificance compared to an Indian business tycoon; albeit Daddy's money.

He quickly washed up his glass and plate, said goodbye to Mr. & Mrs. Dalgety, Selena's only guests this weekend, and headed home.

****

Selena's SLK was not made for Barrington-Jones' drive as she meandered her way up to the homestead. Hudson moved from paw to paw trying to sure up his standing, all the while looking at Selena, most likely thinking she was a crap driver. The two never made eye contact, Selena's leather gloved hands firmly fixed to the steering wheel.

The Barrington-Jones property stat perched atop a hill with commanding views over the valley, the site of the future Oasis 18 hole championship golf course. The property was previously owned by Ben Charlton, his inheritance of the one-hundred-year-old family estate, until he went through a bitter divorce.

Rumors flooded the town at the time of the sale that Mumbai Murray had smooched poor old Ben into selling him the property for a fraction of its true worth promising him 'Glencairn' would remain a family home. Some say Barrington- Jones had submitted a development application to council even before the ink had dried on the contract.

Selena parked her car in front of the front stairs leading onto the verandah. With the sun setting, Selena took a moment to soak up the night air and cast her eye over the property.

The Country Club would sit pride and place on the hill adjacent to the existing homestead which would be eventually demolished. Hudson had perched himself on the window sill, his nose twitching as the aroma of butter chicken fill the air.

Selena knocked on the solid red cedar front door, enriched by hundreds of years of paint and an apt stained-glass panel depicting a green, grassy valley, it had probably welcomed may guests in its lifetime, some very influential no doubt, dodgy or otherwise. But today it would be Selena, delivery woman of forty of the region's best butter chicken lunches. But no reply came from inside.

Hudson, who had decided not to pressure himself with climbing the four steps, barked to let Mumbai Murray know that he had visitors. Two more barks, each a little louder, still met with silence.

Selena made her way to the rear of the property. A small cottage sat on the cliff, possibly a worker's quarters, an office or both. Mr. Barrington-Jones had mentioned in telephone conversations that he sometimes spent hours in the back hours catching up on paperwork. The front door was slightly ajar and Selena called out "Mr. Barrington-Jones, are you in there?"

The door creaked as Selena pushed it open, still calling for Barrington-Jones. The house felt cold, a little eerie as she entered. A table lamp atop a wall table shone in the hallway. The floorboards squeaked as Selena continued inside. Hudson brought up the rear and took up position on the verandah but did not enter the home.

The dimly lit passage way to the rear of the property exhibited vintage photos of the district on the walls, perhaps left behind by the Charlton family.

They certainly didn't appear to be the taste of the current owner who was described as more 'Gold Coast spiv' than a gentleman of the land. The property's coldness and lack of light made Selena assume Barrington-Jones was a frugal man. The oriental hall runners were faded and threadbare.

The office door was open. Selena stepped inside, switched on the light, to reveal papers strewn all over the desk and onto the floor. Hudson barked loudly having lost sight of his minder. He tore around the rear of the property, his barks getting louder and more frequent.

"What's the matter Hudson? Calm down boy"

Selena made her way towards the kitchen. Hudson who had made his way around to the back of the house, could be seen through the flyscreen door still barking. The hair on his spine was raised and his barks were more guttural growls. He was fixated on the floor behind the kitchen table.

Selena followed his eyes down to the floor and behind the table. There she could see a body, lying face down on the linoleum floor, a pool of dried blood solidified under him.

It was Murray Barrington-Jones, her would be customer, now a very dead Mumbai Murray.

Selena raced back to her car; Hudson was in hot pursuit. She reached with one hand into her handbag, shaking as she frantically searched for her mobile phone while the other comforted Hudson.

"Siri, call Detective Cameron Stewart". There was no way she could have dialed the number.

CHAPTER 2

Selena dropped her head into her hands; the distant sirens were getting closer. Looking up she could see a patrol car speeding up the driveway with Detective Cameron Stewart following close behind.

The cars stopped suddenly, stirring up the dust which caused Selena to cough as she directed the officers around the back of the house. A blank stare encompassed her as she took Detective Stewart's advice to remain in her car, along with Hudson, and keep the doors locked.

"Stay here and keep safe. The police surgeon, Dr. Kumar, will be along soon. Can you point him in the right direction?" Stewart remarked, sensitive to Selena's ordeal. Two of the officers went with Stewart, the others in the opposite direction to surround the house; their guns drawn.

A few minutes later Dr. Vijay Kumar arrived in the most gorgeous green vintage Ambassador. The car was a complete contrast to the doctor though, who emerged neck button undone; tie skewwhiff and supporting a two-day growth. Through bloodshot eyes he asked Selena where to go.

She thought back to bed, but pointed around the side of the house to the cottage at the rear. Dr. Kumar was a similar age to her father, but that's where the similarities definitely stopped. In fact, she thought he was a blight on the medical fraternity, let alone her heritage.

17

Sitting in the car gave Selena time to think. Mumbai Murray was a controversial character. His proposed golf course development had its detractors. There would be no shortage of suspects for his killing, but pinpointing that actual killer maybe more difficult.

Her mind was racing as a kaleidoscope of faces passed through her mind, only to be interrupted by snoring coming from Hudson, who was catching fifty winks while all the commotion outside was passing him by.

Detective Stewart returned with Dr. Kumar, a waft of body odor announcing his arrival. "Can you tell us Selena was there anything suspicious you noticed when you arrived?"

"No Detective. I knocked on the front door and called for Mr. Barrington-Jones but there was no answer"

"So, you didn't go inside, touch anything?"

18

"Just the front door. I tried to peer through the stained-glass panel, but I couldn't see anything. It was starting to get dark anyway"

"I remembered when speaking to Murray that he sometimes worked from the cottage at the rear of the main house, so I walked around"

"And Hudson?" to which Dr. Kumar gave an inquisitive look. "My dog. Selena had brought him along for a ride" Stewart finished, looking a bit sheepish.

"He was barking a little" Selena replied her eyes flicking between Stewart and Dr. Kumar. "The place was in darkness but I could see a light in the hallway. I went inside calling his name. I must admit I felt a little scared. It was quite eerie and cold. I found his office down the passage way on the right, so I knocked and went in. Papers were strewn everywhere. That's when Hudson really started going off."

"So he was in the house with you?" Detective Stewart asked. Kumar on the other hand rocked on his heels; his eyes looking around the property.

"As I was saying Dr. Kumar", keen to have him rejoin the conversation, "Hudson had raced around to the back kitchen door and was barking loudly, sort of a guttural sound, more of a growl. When I came to check on him, that's when I noticed Mr. Barrington-Jones on the floor, face down in a pool of dried blood"

"Thank you, Ms. Sharma, you've been most helpful" the doctor replied in a dismissive tone. "I'll get back to the body and send you my report Detective first thing tomorrow."

"Oddball" quipped Stewart after Kumar was out of range. "He's been on a downward spiral ever since his wife left him, but he is thorough" Detective Stewart assured Selena who still was not convinced.

"Did he have a wife, family?" Selena asked.

"Susan Barrington-Jones moved away about three years ago and reverted to her maiden name, Delahunty. Brendan, their son, lives with his mother in Broadwater. I did him for assault for few months back. You remember the Anita Singh case? It was in all the papers"

"Yes, she was pregnant as I recall. Marvelous he is still alive. Raj Singh is a fierce protector of his family. You've got your hands full with this one Detective. Did Mr. Barrington-Jones ever divorce Susan?"

"I'm not sure. I'll check around. She might be the new owner of the Oasis Country Club and golf course. If it gets built now; which reminds me? I best call the contractor and stop his workers coming here tomorrow. I don't want them trouncing over a crime scene"

"I'll leave that in your capable hands Detective Stewart" Selena continued in a formal tone, keeping up appearances in front of his colleagues, not that anything was going on mind you. "I need to clean the slobber out of my car, thanks to Hudson, and get back to my guests."

The drive home was introspective. *Who benefits from Barrington-Jones being dead? Is Susan still his wife? Could Brendan be involved in his father's death? He does have a hot temper.*

Thankfully the Dalgety's had organized their own dinner. A cup of tea, a piece of toast and an early night suited Selena. Tomorrow, she needed to be bright eyed and bushy tailed. A murder needed solving, with or without her formal invite.

CHAPTER 3

With the Dalgety's leaving early, Selena decided to treat herself with an early morning coffee at Jenna's. Armed with her iPad, she jumped into her car and drove into town. Stopping at the zebra crossing she noticed the Pottsville Bakehouse was a buzz with tradies stocking up on sausage rolls and pies as they headed off to work.

Selena smiled that even though she had been in Australia for quite a number of years, she still had not got used to a laborers diet of pies and coke, especially at 6.30am. But there again her Aussie mates would be mortified by eating curry and rice at a similar time like her father's workers in his rice factory. Such is our multicultural world Selena thought as she finally pulled up outside Jenna's.

Jenna greeted Selena with "I'll be with you in a moment, gorgeous" as she finalized placing the sugar containers on the last few tables. Jenna was ex-Melbourne, the home of Australian coffee, and she liked to sprout her expertise on the topic although not always agreed to by the locals. Her forthrightness had caused a bit of backlash on social media with a few harsh critics crucifying her business with bad reviews. But for Selena this was the best coffee house in town and she admired strong opinionated people, especially women just like her.

"What's going on out at the Barrington-Jones place? I believe 'Mumbai Murray' is dead" Jenna enquired, her hands on hips exposing a belly ring from under her t-shirt.

"My, news travels fast here" Selena replied resting her iPad on the table.

"And you found the body"

"Yes. I had a delivery there late yesterday afternoon. Detective Stewart is looking after the case now"

"Obviously you're not a suspect then" Jenna smiled. "What can I get you?"

"Hmm I'm feeling a bit peckish this morning. I'll have your spicy burrito and a skinny flat white" Selena ordered handing back the menu to Jenna. She began scanning Facebook when Detective Stewart walked in and invited himself to sit down.

"Detective you look like…."

"Shit, yes I feel it. I spent most of last night tracking Susan Delahunty down to let her know what had happened to her ex. Finally, about midnight I got hold of Brendan,

25

although he didn't show a lot of emotion over the phone. And when I finally got to sleep, I was woken by Hudson's snoring and a few trips to let him out to relieve himself. What did you feed that dog? Curry?"

"Jenna, I'll have what Selena is having, just go easy on the chili" Stewart ordered glancing over at Pete, the short order cook, whose tats looked more jailhouse than designer ink shop. Maybe he was just naturally suspicious. Being a policeman can do that."

"I imagine there'll be a big turnout at Barrington-Jones's funeral Detective. Not because people will be sad, he's gone, but because they'll be happy, he got his just desserts" Pete piped up while keeping a watchful eye of his bubbling beans.

"You know something about Mr. Barrington-Jones's death Pete?" Stewart enquired.

"No Detective, just commenting on popular sentiment around here" as Pete refocused on scrambling the eggs to put the finishing touches on his diner's burritos.

Mumbai Murray was certainly not the most popular person in town. Stewart would have his hands full trying to sort out who was the murderer. It seemed the whole town was full of suspects.

Ian Carlton, resident grump and self-proclaimed 'mayor' of Pottsville walked in and barked an order to Jenna. He was not her favourite customer and she secretly wished he'd join the bakehouse devotees, but no such luck.

As the local real estate agent and long-term resident, he did have influence in Pottsville although she had wondered if he was behind her scathing reviews on TripAdvisor. But at seventy-five, she doubted he knew how to turn a computer on let alone post a review. And what's TripAdvisor? Carlton would still be a travel agent kind of guy; definitely not an online booking man.

"When do you need the muffins today Mr. Carlton?" Jenna asked with a false smile.

"I'll pick them up at four thirty. I'll need a dozen for tonight's meeting. No, make it two dozen. We may get a few extra along tonight especially as Mumbai Murray won't be attending". Carlton left with a smile and proceeded down the street to his real estate agency. Tonight's town hall meeting was going to be lively.

Stewart finished off his breakfast and wished Selena a pleasant day. He was a bit worse for wear but crime never rests. He would need to press on. Selena felt partly responsible for her Detective's bad night sleep but Indian dogs liked spicy samosas. Hudson would just have to get used to them.

"Oh Detective, if I were you, I'd pay a visit to the Blue Hills Retirement Village in Mooball. Ask for Brian Brady. He and a few of his cronies often grumbled about how Barrington-Jones ripped them off and confined them to the poor house" Pete tossed in.

Stewart nodded his thanks leaving Selena to ponder Pete's accusations. "Another flat white please Jenna" as Selena mulled over the comment while pretending to be scanning her Facebook timeline.

CHAPTER 4

Hudson rode 'shotgun' forcing Selena into the back seat of Detective Stewart's Landcruiser as they headed out of town toward Mooball. About fifteen kilometers out, Stewart took a sharp left down a crooked road, complete with potholes. Hudson adjusted his footing as Stewart attempted to miss the larger holes, although not always successful.

Mooball was a one street town. A garage and general store appropriately covered in spots to represent cows; was the welcoming sign you had arrived. The store had a few tourists who had ventured along the Tweed scenic drive and were sampling it's famous 'super burger'; a bargain at $15 and one not too many people had conquered.

Blue Hills Retirement Village was about four hundred meters from the center of town situated on the flat and in desperate need of a paint job. The welcoming sign was perched at an angle and was just visible above the grass. Selena looked around and realized that this was no pleasure palace. A cool breeze tickled the back of her neck; this place was eerie. The sooner they could leave the better. Even Hudson was happy to stay put in the truck.

"We're looking for Brian Brady" Stewart asked the receptionist, a woman in her late sixties, possibly a resident, who greeted her guests with a blank stare. Selena gave Stewart an inquisitive look as the receptionist dialed for Mr. Brady.

Brian Brady appeared a few minutes later panting, disheveled and wearing a stained Bonds vest, grey track pants and flip flops. "Thanks Moira" he replied to the receptionist who returned her now familiar blank stare.

"We would like to chat to you about Murray Barrington-Jones" Stewart asked after introducing himself and Selena. Brady gruffed and gestured they head back to his cabin.

Brady's cabin reflected the standard of the village. His small porch was crowded with a clothes airer, a dead palm and a three-piece table set, at which they sat leaving Detective Stewart standing room on the stairs.

"I believe you and the some of the residents here had dealings with Mr. Barrington-Jones over the years" Stewart asked.

"One-sided dealings Detective. That crook put us in this dump" Brady replied looking around at the surroundings. Selena glanced at Stewart.

"What do you mean?"

"Detective, myself and a few others owned the land next to Ben Charlton's place. We tried to sell it a few years ago thinking that Ben, rest his soul, might have bought it. We thought it had development potential and we'd make a killing. It was going to be our retirement nest egg"

"But it wasn't?" Selena chimed in.

"No love. It definitely wasn't. Old man Charlton was selling his place around the same time. Enter 'Mumbai Murray' who slimed his way into buying the joint on the proviso the property was to remain a private home. Ben Charlton would turn in his grave if he knew what Barrington-Jones had planned."

"So that partly skedaddled our potential sale as a development site. Then that prick Mumbai Murray played his ultimate card."

"What do you mean?" Stewart asked.

"The mongrel told us that our land was contaminated. Full of pesticides and poisons when the property was used as a dairy farm. It was worthless."

"Didn't you get the soil tested?" Selena asked.

"Murray 'bloody' Barrington-Jones produced a soil test certificate from the Council confirming the ground was contaminated." Brady replied with evil across his face. "But the certificate was false. We found out years later he had paid Reed, a clerk in the Council, to falsify the document, but we couldn't prove it. It was just hearsay and when Reed took his own life, the case was effectively closed.

"So, what happened to the land?" Stewart asked.

"We sold it to Barrington-Jones for less than we paid for it. The banks were up our ribs and Murray was the only buyer. We were left with a huge debt, forcing us to sell everything before the bank closed on us. So instead of sitting at Ocean Shores playing golf and sipping margaritas, we were confined to this dump" Brady bitterly concluded.

"Hmmm that is a sad story Mr. Brady. I can understand your resentment towards Mr. Barrington-Jones. We'll be on our way, but before we go, do you own a rifle?" Stewart asked glaring at Brian Brady.

"No Detective. But I wish I did". Brady dropped his head, the pain of Barrington-Jones rip-off evident. He stood, rubbed his back, bid the detectives good bye and shuffled back into his cottage with the fly screen banging against the timber door frame.

****

Selena jumped into Cameron Stewart's 4wd, still confined to the rear seat thanks to Hudson, as they left the retirement village and headed back to Pottsville.

"What did you make of that?" Stewart asked.

"Every reason to kill a man. Mr. Brady is reminded everyday of what Barrington-Jones did to him. It can't be easy." Selena pondered. "he says he doesn't own a rifle but most men from the land usually do. He was a bit too quick in answering your question, Cameron"

CHAPTER 5

"Cameron, could we drop into Judy Doyle's place? It's just a few hundred meters up here on the left. I like to check-in on her when I can" Selena asked, her head cocked to the right and her big brown eyes melting the Detective into a yes. There was another reason for the visit. She wanted her artist friend to cast her eye over the handsome Detective Stewart, a topic of discussion between the two in the past.

"I guess so" as Stewart entered Ms. Doyle's property causing Selena to beam. Hudson picked up on her excitement and let out an approving bark.

Susan was in her front garden perched in front of a row of hibiscus scrubs which formed a nice tropical hedge to the east of the property. With a canvas taking central place, Susan was adding the final touches to her latest masterpiece.

Judy had moved from Port Douglas in north Queensland a few years ago and purchased her lifestyle hobby farm on the outskirts of Pottsville. A woman in her mid-fifties, divorced and independent, Judy kept to herself. She exhibited a few paintings in a local Byron Bay gallery but outside of opening nights, she rarely socialized with the locals. She did attend a cooking class with Selena and the two women formed a respectful bond from there.

"Hi Judy" an enthusiastic Selena chanted, jumping out of the rear seat of Detective Stewart's 4wd and opening the front passenger door to let Hudson out to stretch his short stumpy legs. Cameron Stewart turned off the engine and quickly joined Selena making their way across the manicured lawn to the hibiscus hedge.

"WOW Judy, this looks almost life like. You've really captured the colours" Selena burst out, hard to contain her genuine approval of Judy's work.

"Thank you darling. It needs a few more touches" as Judy cast her critical eye her painting then looked back at strange man standing next to Selena and his four-legged panting friend.

"Sorry you haven't met Detective Stewart before, have you? And this is Hudson" Selena commented with a glint in her eye. Judy immediately remembered some of their late-night conversations but played a poker face to Mr. Stewart. He was different than what she expected. Perhaps a little meek and mild but there again a nice balance for a very forthright Selena she thought.

"So, what brings you out this way young lady?" Judy asked as she washed her hands in the kitchen sink and gesturing the couple to take a seat at the dining table.

"Detective Stewart and I have just been to the Blue Hills retirement village and we were on our way back to Pottsville, so we thought we would call in"

"You thought you would call in. I doubt if the poor detective here had a choice" Judy smiled knowing full well Selena's domineering nature would have ruled the passage home, even if she was a back seat passenger.

"Your dog, Hudson, won't eat my prize Hibiscus's, will he?" momentarily taking her eyes off a dashing Hudson to stare back at Detective Stewart.

"No, unless they smell like lamb chops Ms. Doyle" the detective replied.

"Oooh he is formal, Selena. I can see we are going to have to relax this one, eh" as Judy flipped the lid off the kettle to add some water for their tea.

Cameron Stewart looked puzzled as his mind filled with thoughts of what other men Selena had brought to Judy's house. But with a shake such thoughts were dismissed as Cameron being silly. While he and Selena worked well together on cases, they had never been out on an actual date. In his mind he had no right to think suck thoughts, but it did needle him a little. Could there have been?

"I'm guessing you're on the Barrington-Jones case Detective?" Judy asked as she set the table for tea, rummaging the bottom of the biscuit jar to find something give to her guests. "I feel like old Mrs. Hubbard today" as the jar gave up nothing.

41

"I don't need a cookie, Judy. My waistline is telling me I need to cut back. Selena is always offering up some delicacies. Hudson loves her curry puffs" Stewart replied causing Judy to frantically to look outside at her beautifully manicured lawn hoping Hudson hadn't left a nasty deposit.

"Yes, he is on the case and I'm his trusty assistant" a beaming Selena added.

"He was a weird one" Judy continued as she poured the tea. His poor wife, well ex-wife"

"What do you mean?" Selena asked.

"You know she had an affair with Tommy Llewellyn?"

"Really, the photographer in Bangalow. How do you know that, Judy?" Selena asked knowing that Ms. Doyle was not the most social person in the district and she couldn't see her chin wagging with a bunch of gossips over coffee.

"It was pretty well known around these parts. Let's just say there was a different kind of exposure going on in Llewellyn's dark room than just negatives being developed. Tommy is a lady's man. Very well connected. In fact, his father used to trade a lot in your country Selena. I think Tommy may have been the cause of Murray and Susan splitting" Judy explained.

"But that's just talk; isn't it Judy? Rumors in a small town are rife at the best of times. Most people think the Detective and I are dating" Selena threw in at the last moment to give Cameron Stewart a jolt.

"What?" Stewart retorted only to see Selena laugh uncontrollably.

"Don't worry Detective. My father would have you killed if such a rumor floated back to India. Heaven help us if we lost our one and only detective around here."

"Maybe an opening for 'Detective' Sharma" Judy threw in noticing Stewart was squirming in his seat. "But on a serious note, Murray came to see me about a week ago. He had commissioned me to do some paintings for his new clubhouse. He was a little stressed then. He mentioned he was trying to finalise his divorce with Susan. Something that needed doing before the clubhouse got underway"

"I wonder if Susan knew of his intentions. A divorce would cut her out of a potential fortune?" Stewart remarked.

"No idea Detective. Not sure how far advanced he was with the whole thought. Why do you ask?"

"It would seem a pretty dam good motive for murder, I would think"

" Hmmm, I guess so but that's why you are the detective Mr. Stewart" Judy replied with a patronizing look. "I'm going to need to move you good folk out of my house. I have a friend coming over for dinner and I need to start preparing dinner."

"A good friend?" Selena enquired, digging a little deeper. "That wouldn't be Carol, would it?"

"You never cease to amaze me, Miss Selena. Cooking school queen, part time detective and now.....matchmaker?" Judy smiled. "Perhaps you'd like to join us, Selena. I'm sure the good detective can find his way home"

No, no I best be on my way too" Selena replied, slightly panicking about the thought of spending an intimate dinner with Judy and Carol, but knowing Judy was only teasing. "Come on Hudson, time to go"

Hudson appeared from the side of the house wearing one of his best 'have you forgot something' looks. Judy immediately picked up on it and fetched a couple of meatballs from the fridge, leftovers from the night before.

"I hope the Italian spices don't upset Hudson on the way home in the car" Judy laughed.

"Nah, Selena has been feeding him her famous curry puffs lately. He's almost Indian" Cameron quipped looking fondly down at Hudson who was totally oblivious to his adoring looks. "But we'll keep the windows down just in case."

CHAPTER 6

Selena arrived home to an empty house. Her new guests had left a note that had slipped down to Cabarita Beach for fish and chips and not to wait up as they had their key.

Fish and chips sounded divine. This had become one of Selena's comfort foods since moving to Australia. Rosie's at Caba knew where to source the freshest fish and their batter was ever so light; almost like tempura batter. Selena reminisced about the times she would sit on a park bench in front of the surf club and savior Rosie's hot, crisp chips.

But not tonight. She smiled thinking that her guests were probably grateful not to be eating curry although she could never understand why the English insisted on drowning perfectly crisp chips in vinegar. Yuck! She couldn't think of anything worse. There again the Poms would probably scratch their heads over Indians flooding chips with curry sauce. Each to their own Selena thought.

Beachside cafes in Goa had great fish and curry sauce. As a little girl, Selena would often go for her school holidays to Goa. She had fond memories of sitting with her dad snacking on fish curry while overlooking the ocean. They were peaceful times. Her Dad seemed so relaxed and her Mum appreciated a cooking free break as well.

They were simple times when being a school girl came with little pressure, at least from her father. Sure, there was always pressure to do well at school but her father rarely spoke about his business and that one-day Selena would run it. It's a pity that was no son in the family. Selena's heir apparent status would be removed. She would much rather be the 'Prince Harry' of her rice royalty family.

The fridge looked a little bare. A nice cup of tea along with a healthy slice of salted caramel pie would be dinner tonight.

Selena cocked herself in her comfy verandah chair and soaked up the evening sky. The serenity was one of the most enduring things about her home; another reason why she wouldn't want to return to India and be bombarded with the constant horn blasts by passing motorcycles.

Selena mulled the day's activities around in her head. She felt a little sad for Murray Barrington – Jones finding out his wife was having an affair with Tommy Llewellyn. Could there be any 'studio' shots in his dark room. Susan by all encounter didn't seem to be the type to stray, but you never really know what some people would do behind closed doors.

And what about the betrayal. How long had the affair been going on? How did it become exposed? What would have the hurt been like?

Selena hoped that she would never have to go through such pain. This is another reason why she would never return home to marry her father's preferred choice; he looks like a right pratt.

But Cameron Stewart, on the other hand. Hmmmm. Selena could see an eternity of happiness with Detective Stewart.

Selena laughs out loud at the comment Cameron made about Susan Barrington-Jones and Tommy Llewellyn "Old Susan was doing a bit of horizontal folk dancing with

Tommy, eh" Aussies, she thought, they have some strange sayings.

Her Earl Grey tea was going down very nicely tonight. The Barrington-Jones' divorce was still a bit of a puzzle to Selena.

Did the affair really cause the divorce? Rumours around town were that Murray had a huge life insurance policy over himself where his son would be the sole beneficiary. Three million bucks was the touted amount by 'looses lips' Lonergan, the local AMP insurance rep.

As for the house, Susan would become the estate owner. Murray wasn't pleased with her 'little stray' but he thought she should be in a position to comfortably look after their son. It would seem Murray still had the flame burning for Susan.

Selena looked down at her watch. 9.05pm was not too late to ring her friend Cameron.

She had a few questions that needed answering otherwise she would sleep.

Cameron was walking around his house turning off the lights, hot chocolate in one hand and a Tim Tam delicately poised in his mouth so as not to melt the chocolate coating when the phone rang.

"Oh, it's Selena. What could she possibly want at this hour" Cameron thought hitting the green button?

"Good evening my little curry puff" Cameron cheekily answered. Selena smiled taking his remark as a compliment, a sign that they might be getting a little closer. Cameron didn't have the same romantic thoughts, instead thinking he could use their familiarity to cast a bit of whit.

"Glad you're still up Detective. I picked you for a hot chocolate and slippers man ready for bed at 9pm" It was almost as if Selena was a fly on the wall as Cameron glared menacingly at the mosquito buzzing around his bedroom.

"I've just been thinking about Murray's divorce and will" Selena pausing to gather her thoughts.

"And Ms. Detective" Cameron quipped.

"If Murray was going to divorce Susan, officially I mean, why would he keep her in the will?"

"Well, there's a bit more to it than that" Cameron reluctantly replied considering how much he should divulge to Selena and if this conversation could come back to bite him.

"Can you keep a secret?" Cameron nervously replied, and rightfully so. Selena hadn't kept a secret since she learned little Indian girls were not made from sugar n spice. She was three then.

"I had a chat with Peter Carter, Murray's solicitor. He couldn't break his client's confidentiality relationship but since Mr. Barrington-Jones had now passed, he let me into a few things"

"Go on" Selena eagerly dived in, sitting on the edge of her seat, the tea and pie safely perched on the side table. She was all ears.

"The Will says that if Murray and Susan ever divorced, she would be cut from the will. She'd get nothing. Susan and Brendan would only collect on Murray's death" Cameron informed Selena still wondering if by opening his mouth he would end up being bitten on the arse.

"That's interesting. And now Murray is dead; that puts Susan and Brendan squarely in the frame. Did Murray ever serve divorce papers to Susan?" Selena asked.

"On the morning of Murray's death. Peter Carter served the papers" Cameron replied.

"And I'm guessing she wasn't too pleased about that" Selena feeling the sting of the message the divorce papers screamed at Susan.

"She went ballistic" according to Carter. "She raged about being penniless, not being able to live and not having money to support Brendan" Cameron went on.

"Sounds like a pretty good motive for murder Detective, wouldn't you say. Not that I'm an expert. You are the Detective here in this scenario" Selena added with a bit of tongue in cheek.

"And that I am Miss Cooking School owner, and we should stick to our professions. Agreed? Besides it's getting late and I'm off to bed."

"There's just one thing that's bothering me though Cameron. Let's say Susan did kill Murray. Where does that put Brendan? One parent dead and the other in prison. Not ideal, is it?" Selena speculated.

"I guess a murderer doesn't go through every possible scenario around their forthcoming actions. A lot of these things occur on impulse. They're not planned. Things just get out of hand. As I said 25 minutes ago, I'm off to bed Selena. And by the way, the snoring you can hear, that's Hudson. Judy's meatballs knocked him out."

"Speaking of Judy, she's having dinner with Carol tonight, you know, the massage therapist two doors away from Charlton's real estate shop. I must give Judy a call in the morning"

"There you go again, sticking your nose in" Cameron replied trying to get off the phone politely. "And from what I've heard, Carol the masseuse, bats for the other team."

"She didn't always. She was married with two kids. Then one day she decided that she wanted to put herself first, broke the news to the family and moved up here from Melbourne. I believe everything is fine with the family and the kids often come up here to see her. I'm pretty sure her and Judy have a lot in common."

The cogs in Cameron's brain were turning ever so slowly but he finally put two and two together.

"Selena, there you go again getting yourself involved in other people's lives. Stick to your cooking please."

"Oh 100% Detective. I'm just keeping your…..how does your favourite Detective Hercule Poirot say it….*little grey cells turning*. Good night"

CHAPTER 7

Selena meandered down the main street of Pottsville casually looking about and soaking up the morning sun. It was a beautiful morning. Selena would never experience such serenity in India. The nose from two stoke motor bikes and the constant ringing of horns kept one in a permanent state of mild anxiety.

The doors from Peter Carter's office swung open and two people rushed on the street in front of Selena almost knocking her down. Her quiet enjoyment was broken and she felt a little shaken as she clutched her heart and pulled her bag close to her. She stopped in her track

The intruding couple stormed towards a parked Toyota; their faces filled with rage with the man cursing "arsehole". Selena stared. Not even an apology for their barging rudeness nor one coming as the car reversed into the oncoming traffic causing a screech of brakes and gorks from passersby.

Diane Brown, Peter Carter's secretary came rushing onto the street.

"Are you ok Selena?" she asked.

"Yes, nearly got mowed down by Susan… umm…aagh…Delahunty and some bloke" Selena replied in a shaken voice.

"Tommy Llewellyn" Diane said filling in the missing piece for Selena.

"Didn't look to happy and left in quite a rush. Nearly had a prang"

"No, they weren't" Diane replied looking about to see if anybody was in close proximity and if she was best by prying eyes.

"I shouldn't be telling you this but"

Selena jumped in and stopped Diane in her tracks. "Don't tell me client secrets and get yourself and Mr. Carter in trouble" Selena remarked looking Diane squarely in the eye and gesturing with her hand to stop, while at the same time hoping Diane would weaken and spill everything. She didn't have to wait long.

"Susan just collected Murray's will. Even though Peter had served divorce papers on her, it was never finalized"

"So, she gets everything" Selena commented with an inquisitive face recalling the conversation she had with Detective Stewart the night before.

"Not quite. If he died of natural causes everything would go to Brendan"

"So, she was out?"

"Yes, but if he died from misconduct, both she and Brendan would be out"

"Interesting. So, who is the beneficiary now?" Selena asked.

"Can't tell you that. I best get back into the office. Peter will be wondering where I am"

Selena headed towards Jenna's coffee shop when she felt a slip between her upper body and arm pulling her faster down the street. It was Judy with a determined look on her face.

"Morning Jude. Where are we off to in such a hurry?" Selena enquired with a puzzled look while trying to free her arm. While she does have dark skin, she does bruise easily and Judy did have a firm grip.

"I've got some interesting news" guiding Selena to a quiet corner in Jenna's café.

"You and Carol.....moving in together? Getting married?"

"Sshh, sshh. There's no time for your matchmaking today Ms. Selena. I found out something interesting last night" Judy remarked while gesturing to Jenna for two coffees.

Selena kept quiet. She could see Judy had something important to say.

"You know who Annie Greer is, right? She's that conservationist activist, some say nutter. She's married to Paul Greer, the State Environment Minister.

Well, she had learned that at the back of Barrington- Jones' property is a koala habitat spreading along the boundary into the land Brady and his cronies used to own.

She was lobbying with the local greenies to get a heap of signatures onto a petition to stop the development altogether. I think she was going to pressurize her husband to block the development going ahead; override the Council's ruling."

"WOW that would have put a spanner in the works" Selena replied. "Was she getting the support?"

"Not sure. She's got a bit of pull around here, especially with the Byron crowd. She'd protest in a one-horse race just for the sake of it".

"And hubby? Is he very active in her issues?" Selena asked.

"Spends most of his time in Sydney even when Parliament isn't sitting. Couldn't blame him I suppose. Annie would drive you bonkers?

The two women chatted some more but as the café started to fill, they decided to abandon their private conversation before it became public.

"I'll let Cameron know. It'll add another dimension to his investigation. I can't see Annie the greenie being a murderer but I guess I don't know what some people will do to 'save the koalas.'"

"Good idea. And then you can get back to your cooking 'Miss India'" Judy remarked looking deeply into Selena's eyes knowing full well she'd use this tid bit to cement herself firmly into the case.

CHAPTER 8

Selena jumped into her Mercedes sports car fighting an annoying voice in the back of her mind. Leave it to Detective Stewart. He's the policeman. Leave it to him.

But Selena couldn't do that. She had been fighting similar conversations all her life and she wasn't about to give into this nagging little voice today.

She did a u-turn in the main street bringing a Holden Colorado to a sudden holt which she validated as the driver was going too fast. The tradie wasn't too impressed by Selena thought it was a woman's prerogative to do such things and that men need to fall into line.

With a smile she continued towards Annie Greer's place. She knew that back in India she could never get away with such tactics especially if she succumbed to her father's wishes and married her arranged husband to be. In India women are thought of as second-class citizens especially by the older generation although there are some changes to that thinking afoot.

Arriving at Annie's house, Selena noticed her husband Paul was in the front yard pruning a few trees. He could be there for a lifetime she thought.

To say the landscape was 'a-la-natural' would be an understatement. The hedge was overgrown with branches peering through the picket fence. A passionfruit vine was out of control along the side and the grass could do with a mow.

So, this is what being a conservationist is about Selena thought as she approached the gate telling herself that she won't be enlisting any time soon. She's a pruned hedge, manicured lawn type of girl.

"Good morning Mr. Greer" Selena said greeting a startled grey-haired man, slight frame and white pasty skin supporting a three day beard growth. With his mouth wide opened Paul Greer looked like a politician who had his hand caught in the government coffers and had just been busted for a travel rort.

"I'm Selena Sharma. I've got the cooking school down the road"

Paul Greer's look went from a guy about to have a mild heart attack to one of being stunned. *Who is this girl? Do I know her? Did I*

*have a little dalliance with an Indian lady in the past
and this is her daughter?*

"I was hoping Annie was in. I wanted to chat to her about koalas in the area. I hear she's an expert" Selena remarked noticing some colour was returning to Mr. Greer's face and the beginnings of a smile had started to replace his gaping open mouth. The man looked positively relieved.

"Yes, she's in. Come on through. Mind your step on the broken concrete path. I've been meaning to fix that for years" Paul said gesturing towards the front door of the house while calling for Annie at the same time.

"Annie, you've got a visitor. It's that nice girl from the cooking school"

Looking through the open door, the house took on a style similar to the landscaping; natural. The house appeared dark, perhaps the curtains were drawn. No lights appeared

on but there again the lady was a conservationist.

A grey-haired woman shuffled her
Birkenstocks along the lino towards the front
door. Annie was no modern-day fashionista;
very much stuck in the late sixties, early
seventies. The look was easily recognisable to
Selena. There was a small tribe of what Selena
had heard Cameron Stewart describe as 'the
hairy armpit brigade' in Pottsville and it
appeared that Annie was a fully paid-up card-
carrying member.

Hello Annie, it's been a while. I was just
passing and wanted to say hi and perhaps
have a little chat?"

"Selena, you look magnificent. Of course,
come in but I will have to rush off soon.
I've got to deliver a talk at the town hall
soon. Those bloody money hungry,
capitalist bastard developers are scaring all

the koalas away" Annie replied, opening the fly screen door and inviting Selena into the house, suggesting she moves to the rear of the house where the kitchen was located.

Selena sat at the old wooden kitchen table which looked like it housed a thousand stories. The chair had seen better days but it was still solid. *They don't make things like this anymore Selena* thought; a saying often sprouted by her father particularly when fondling talking about his '62 Rolls Royce. He could easily afford a new one, but the '62 model had real heritage for the business man. Selena remembered her father regularly thumbing the coffee table book about the origin of Rolls Royce.

Annie presented Selena with a cup of instant coffee. "Sugar, milk dear?" It had been a while since Selena had 'instant coffee'. She wasn't even sure it was still being sold in stores any more, but it must. Ever since her arrival in Australia, Selena had refined her taste of coffee to the extent of being referred to as a 'Melbourne coffee snob". But she wasn't here for the coffee.

"Tell me more about the koala habitats in the area Annie?"

"Everybody thinks we have millions of them, especially the Yanks. But that's simply not the case. They are a dying breed and we need to look after them."

"I know what you mean. I had an American couple staying at the guesthouse recently and they thought koalas hung from every tree or lamp post in Australia" Selena commented.

"Exactly. And we would have thousands of them if it wasn't for that mob clearing land around old Murray's property. Bloody murder it is, total carnage and I'm going to stop them! Well try to anyway. I think I might have missed my opportunity but I'm rallying the troops and we're going to give the Council hell"

"You sound very determined Annie. Are you thinking of chaining yourself to the tractors or gum trees?"

"That's what we used to do in the seventies. Remember the French bombing in the Atoll? We gave the frogs their just desserts."

"I was just a bit too slow on this occasion. You probably don't know this but at the bottom of old Charlton's place was an old barn. It used to house old farm machinery. I would often hide in there trying to get photos of the koalas so I could plead my case to Council. But while I was gathering the evidence, the golf course got approved. Too slow these days"

"I can see your passion for the koalas. I hope to chat to you more about them another day. Ill certainly let my guests know of your mission. Perhaps there are more habitats in the area. I won't hold you up. I know you've got to be at the town hall" Selena commented as she gathered her keys and made way to the door.

Where's the old boy" Annie cried out looking for her husband. "Selena is going darling"

"Nice to see you again my dear. Annie and I must come and have one of delicious curries soon. Bye, I'm off to the rifle range"

Annie rolled her eyes. Obviously, she didn't approve of her husband's hobby *strange hobby* Selena thought, for a couple of old hippies, opening the fence gate and walking to her car.

Hudson had sat patiently guarding Selena's car. His panting was audible as Selena got into the driver's seat, causing her to smile and reach across the seat for a 'well done' cuddle.

The drive back home was time to ruminate their conversation. Annie was certainly a passionate woman about preserving wildlife and nature. She certainly had a vicious dislike for "Mumbai" but could she really take it to the next level and kill the man?

Nah, that was stretching things a bit too far. Besides hippies were about peace and love, and not war.

But then there was her gun carrying, rifle range shooting husband. An odd pastime......

CHAPTER 9

Selena sat on her verandah overlooking the green rolling fields, enjoying the serenity while sipping on her favourite brew; a cup of Darjeeling tea. Pottsville was a good catchment area for regular rainfall; hence the fields were green for the best part of the year.

Here mobile phone rang. It was Cameron. A smile appeared on her face as she hit the accept button.

"How's your day going?"

"Just got better" Selena cheekily replied to a blushing Cameron Stewart on the other end of the line.

Getting the conversation back on a business track, Cameron replied "Well I'm off to check on a couple of things about Murray's death with the coroner. I've also booked into see Susan Barrington-Jones later on. She came back for his cremation which I guess was a nice thing to do"

"Or she was just making sure he was really dead and never going to rise from the ashes" Selena chimed in with a pinch of skepticism about her motives.

"There, there Selena. Give her the benefit of the doubt" a softer Detective Stewart replied.

"Maybe. She might have been technically still married to Murray because the papers although served, she was cut out of his will by the fact Mr. Barrington-Jones met with foul play"

"Will, what will? How do you know that?" Cameron quickly rebutted.

"I bumped into Dianne from the solicitor's office. She told me"

"Crikey, talk about loose lips sink ships. No confidentiality in this town is there" a furious Detective Stewart replied shaking his head.

"Dianne used to date Murray before Susan came along. Broke off the relationship over the phone. It broke her heart"

"Yes, I guess it would have. Any other gems of information you've forgotten to tell me Selena?"

"I think this puts Susan right in the frame; being cut out of the will. Wouldn't you agree Cameron?"

"Yes except Susan only found out about her being cut from the will today"

"I guess so. That's why you are the detective and I'm just a cook" Selena replied hoping for a compliment. It didn't come.

"What about Brendan? Could he have known about the will and killed his dad?" Selena suggested.

"Anything is possible but I doubt it. The two of them were pretty close. Even when Brendan and his mother moved away, Brendan would return often and stay with his father. I don't buy it Selena.

"Ok how about Annie Greer. She's very passionate about saving koalas and apparently there was a habitat of them on Murray's property before he started clearing."

"Yes, I know her. I gave her a warning a few years ago about smoking weed on her front porch with her 'environmentalist husband'. The neighbours complained a few times so I had to act. But I didn't fine her. Just to be more mindful of the neighbours."

"Oh that 'environmentalist, gun carrying, rifle shooting husband" Selena dropping in the gun references.

"Didn't know that. Who would have thought" Cameron replied pondering the thought for a moment longer?"

"I don't know if Annie is a shooter but she certainly had her pick of rifles in the house. Paul owned three. She could have borrowed one of his and committed the deadly act" Selena tossing more thoughts in for consideration.

"Worth considering, I guess. I need to run. Let's chat later. Maybe you'll have some more theories by then 'Detective Selena'. Ciao bella" Cameron let slip, smacking his forehead with his hand, not believing he had just said that. It wasn't missed by Selena hanging up the phone with an enormous smile.

CHAPTER 10

Selena woke from a peaceful sleep. The soft early morning sunlight beamed into her bedroom The sheer curtains danced with the light breeze as she stretched, then rolled out of bed. She moved to the kitchen, her bare feet connecting with her timber floors grounding her. The stove top coffee was bubbling away, its aroma filling the house. Selena reminded herself how lucky she was as she gazed across the beautiful Pottsville grass lands.

You could never get such peace and serenity in India she thought but Pottsville did have its drawbacks. Two actually.

She missed her father albeit he can be testing at times. Long chats about their family heritage gave Selena a sense of belonging. They grounded her to know the struggle her father went through to build the family business to what it is today.

It would be easy to return and take over this successful company, but it wouldn't be right. She hadn't felt the struggle, the pain and the pressures from the banks in the early days just to waltz in and be the 'Princess' of the business.

In a small way she was getting her understanding of building her own business here in Australia.

And then there was the other issue with Pottsville; a severe lack of eligible men. There are lots of bachelors within the Indian community in the region, but none appealed to Selena. She had eyes for only one man and with a sigh brought herself back into the day.

Selena quickly changed into a sleeveless silk top, donned a pair of slightly ripped jean shorts, tucked her mobile phone into her back pocket and headed to Jenna's for breakfast.

The towns folk had gathered at Jenna's with the outdoor tables all taken. The takeaway coffee que was robust, so Selena went inside and grabbed the last table in the back corner.

Selena looked at the menu. She was just filling in time. She already knew what she was having. It was the reason she had driven here; scramble eggs on Turkish bread with grilled tomatoes on the side. The only thing she hadn't decided was whether she'd add smoked salmon to the order.

She looked up over the menu and saw Hudson waddling towards her. This brought a smile but her eyes filled with excitement when she saw Cameron Stewart following him, acknowledging a few diners as he passed.

"Morning Ms. Selena" Cameron said with a cheeky smile. "Hudson knew exactly where to find you"

"Oh, were you specifically looking for me Detective?" Selena snapped back with lightning speed; her comment disguised with an air of innocence.

"Selena, Selena, Selena, I thought you'd might like to know about my chat with Dr Kumar last night"

"Was he sober?" Selena had no time for the man. A disgrace to Indian mankind.

"There, there Selena. Murray was shot, nothing new there. But it seems to be from a distance, most probably fired from a high-powered hunting rifle"

"Ok but there must be hundreds of rifles in the area Detective?"

"According to Dr Kumar the distance from where the shot was fired is the key. It had to be high powered, possibly a pump action and the one that fits the bill is a Remington 7600.

"Hmmm nice work but remember Mr. Barrington-Jones was found dead at the rear of his house, inside. There were no broken windows with bullet hoes in them" Selena stated throwing a spanner into Detective Stewarts analysis, causing a bit of disbelief in his theory.

"True, true. But what if Murray was shot outside and dragged into the house?" Stewart replied with a look of 'who's the detective now'

Jenna sided up to the table. "Usual for you gorgeous". Selena smiled handing back the menu. "And you Detective? Coffee? And a sided serve of bacon for Hudson?" Jenna teased. She rushed back to kitchen so Pete could begin Selena's order.

"Anything else from your discussions?" Selena continuing the discussion.

"It appears that Brendan was to get his father's estate, which was the case even if Murray had me with foul play. But he was going to see his mother right. She could stay in the property, rent free."

"Not according to Diane. Somebody else was to get the property?"

"Murray amended the will only last month. Must have had a conscious and decided the property should go to his son after all. Apparently, Carter hadn't got around to attaching the amendment to the will, but it is legal and enforceable"

"So, what about the golf club development?" Selena asked.

"Probably not happening anytime soon. Carter the solicitor is handling that now on behalf of Brendan. The kid by pure nature of his age is a bit whet behind the ears for this sort of thing."

Detective Stewart leaned in across the table. Selena dreamt of a good morning kiss. Cameron Stewart had some more news. Story of my life Selena thought.

"There might be another suspect. A guy called Stefan Rudinski, Chapter President of the Viper Motorcycle Club"

"What?" screeched Selena, enough to turn heads and have Jenna running to their table with breakfast. Hudson woofed a couple of times until he received a reassuring pat from Detective Stewart.

"Susan got a call, out of the blue, from this Rudinski fellow, telling her he was on the way to farm to chat to her. Up the driveway came two Harley Fat Boys, ridden by two heavily tattooed men wearing their club colours.

Rudinski, his face covered in a decorative tattoo, introduced himself and his fellow club member. Apparently, he was in business with Murray; the drug business. Murray would manufacture ecstasy pills, ice and steroids and Stefan and his gang would distribute the candy, as he called it, from Tweed to Ballina"

"I can't believe it Mr. Barrington – Jones involved in drugs. And with bikies!" a stunned Selena replied.

"And it get's worse. Rudinski claims that Murray owes him $500,000 and since he's dead, Susan will have to repay the debt"

"Far out! Where is she going to get that kind of money from?" Selena enquired.

"She was very frightened, as you would be, coming from a heavily tattooed bikie with a thick Russian accent. He summoned his henchman. The guy produced a sawn-off shot gun and placed it against her temple. And pulled the trigger. The gun was empty, thank goodness.

Rudinski laughed then switched back to his threatening mood demanding the cash by the end of the week. He added more pressure by mentioning that Brendan might be the next Barrington-Jones to appear next in the local funeral notices.

"Where on Earth is Susan going to get that sort of money" Selena responded.

"I'll have a little chat with Mr. Rudinski and remind him that he can't collect off an illegal activity. Otherwise, he'll be spending a lengthy time in a 'one bedroom flat overlooking a concrete courtyard. I'm sure Susan won't hear from her Russian friend again.

Anyway, I best be off. I've got a few things I need to attend to" Cameron said reaching over to Selena's plate, grabbing the toast crusts and tossing them to Hudson who snapped them up like a Hoover vacuum, licking his chops as a seal of approval.

Selena watched her two favourite men leave the café but was soon distracted by an impressive figure, a slim, tanned, grey hair tied on a small man bun, confidently stride into the café. A kiss more than a peck indicated he knew Jenna well.

"Selena, meet a good friend of mine, Simon Fanning". Sion smiled and extended his hand. "Simon runs the Mindfulness Centre in Mullumbimby"

"Nice to meet you" Selena replied feeling somewhat calm just having this man in her presence. His piercing blue eyes, soft but masculine hands and the way he fixated himself on her was very energizing.

Jenna explained what Simon does and how she had been a student of his classes, promoting the lasting benefits of his teachings.

"Perhaps I should attend a few of your classes Simon?" Selena flirted.

"That would be wonderful but I think some one-on-one sessions would be mutually beneficial. Let me know if you're interested and we can set up some times" the charismatic Simon gestured.

Jenna smiled, gave Selena the raised eyebrow of approval, having been a one-on-one 'student' of Simon's before.

CHAPTER 11

Selena headed home, raced into the kitchen and cut herself a large slice of salted caramel cheesecake, placed it into an air tight container and raced back to the car eager to continue her journey.

But it was momentarily slowed. Cameron had pulled up blocking the driveway.

"Would you mind looking after Hudson today? The Chief Super doesn't like dogs at the station and apparently, he's been harassing my next-door neighbour Mrs. Darlington's cat."

"Sure. C'mon Hudson" Selena called opening the passenger the passenger side door. Selena followed Detective Stewart down the driveway turning right onto Cudgen Creek Road and headed towards the Barrington-Jones property.

Her conversation with Annie Greer had been playing on her mind. She had mentioned an abandoned shack on the property, an ideal spot to observe the koala habit. Selena wanted to check it out for herself.

She continued past the property, rounded the bend and parked on the flat. The view back up to the main house was impressive; such a commanding position at the top of the hill delivering sweeping views over the valley.

Selena and Hudson headed towards the clump of trees that bounded the adjoining property. Beautiful eucalyptus gums, tall and firmly rooted into the soil, it would be a shame to knock them over to make way for a golf course. But that was progress.

The ground was a little bit soggy after the downpour the previous night making it damp underfoot and the thick grass more difficult to maneuver especially for Hudson. But he was taking it in his short stumpy stride and the thought of soiling Selena's car probably hadn't entered his mind. In the world of Hudson this was another great day out.

The pair stopped in their tracks. Before them was a dilapidated hut, timber panels mostly rotten, a tin roof with holes the size of cricket balls and the window glass panels shattered. It was in a sorry state, obviously not used for decades.

But it was easy to imagine a thriving meeting place for the early farm workers enjoying shelter from the elements particularly the harsh summer sun. A refreshing brew of coffee and tea, perhaps some damper, and a lively chat about the topic of the day. This place had character and the workers voices could still be heard in the imagination of anybody who stumbled upon her.

Inside the shack cob webs covered the old table and chairs. Resemblance of a camp fire with a billy tea pot above would have been the gathering place, to warm their hands and rest their bodies before returning outside to look after the cows and other farm animals.

Selena continued to look around while Hudson was scratching the dirt floor as if a buried bone had got his attention.

"What are you doing Hudson? Stop digging boy. There are no bones there" Selena stated shaking her head and thinking about muddy paws on the carpet mats of her Mercedes.

Just as well Hudson was Cameron's pride and joy, otherwise he might be accidently forgotten for the trip back home.

Hudson completely ignored Selena. His tiny little legs were going ten to the dozen when he unearthed a dirty, brass coloured object.

"What have you found here boy?" Selena commented with a look of wonder as she stood up and closely inspected the object; a bullet, most likely from a rifle.

Maybe this is the shell from the bullet that killed Murray Barrington-Jones? But why was it still here on the floor. Surely an experienced rifleman would have picked it up. Was the shooter frightened? Did he or she need to get away quickly?

There were many questions that needed answering. Selena gathered up Hudson and ran back to the car brushing his paws as she went. Closing the passenger door with Hudson securely inside, Selena made her way to the driver's seat.

"Shit!" she exclaimed. "A flat tyre!"

Selena looked around. An eerie, cool breeze flowed over her body. She began to shake. Her tyre had been perforated with a sharp object and it was deliberate.

CHAPTER 12

An hour had passed since Selena had phoned the NRMA rep to come and fix her tyre. Hudson helped pass the time, although he was getting a bit restless.

Selena hoped that Hudson didn't need a toilet break as she had no intentions of unlocking the car and letting him out. Maybe it was in the knowing that a murder had occurred here, but the Barrington-Jones farm felt colder today.

Up the driveway came the NRMA van. Finally, Selena thought. I'm getting out of here.

"Flat tyre Miss. We'll have you out of here in a jippy" the mechanic commented as he swagged back to his van to fetch some tools. Within 15 minutes Selena had the damaged tyre in the boot ready for Jimmy to look at it in the morning.

On the way back to her guesthouse, Cameron finally returned her call.

"Well, I was thinking you had forgotten me. Can you pop over? I've got something to show you"

"No Ms. Selena I hadn't forgotten you but as you know crime never sleeps. Are you thinking dinner?" Detective Stewart hinted.

"I suppose I could rustle up a salad" Selena replied, not to enthusiastic about cooking after her ordeal that day.

"Hmmm no butter chicken?" Detective Stewart replied pushing the envelope and Selena's buttons.

Selena counted to ten before she replied "Of course Detective. Just for you. See you around 7pm."

Cameron Stewart arrived promptly at seven, clasping a chilled bottle of Semillon in his right hand. Selena was appreciative of the gesture as she placed it in the fridge.

"Come sit, I've got something to show you"

Stewart looked like a seven-year-old boy filled with anticipation on Christmas Eve as Selena slipped away to her bedroom, returning within seconds with something hidden in her closed fist, plonking the object down on the table with an almighty thump as if she was playing a round of snap.

"WOW! Where did you get this Selena?" Cameron raising his voice to Selena who was back in the kitchen plating up their dinner.

"At the Barrington-Jones property" as she returned to the table placing their meals on the table and pulling her seat in.

"Oh, I nearly forgot the wine. Back in a sec"

Where exactly on the Barrington-Jones property did you find this?"

"Annie told me about an old hut on the property that she and a few of her mates would visit to watch koalas decades ago. It's way down on the boundary hidden by a few trees, pretty decayed, broken window, rusted roof, that type of thing"

Hudson found the bullet shell."

"He's a Stewart through and through" Cameron exclaimed with a smile, but then contained himself. "I'm glad he's not here tonight. He'd be wanting an extra-large bone as a reward"

"Do you think this might be cartridge from the bullet that killed Murray?"

"Well, it is the same, but how far is this hut from the house?"

"I'm guessing a hundred meters, maybe a little more" Selena replied.

"The shooter would need to be a bit of a marksman then. That's a reasonable distance to hit a target, and in this case, the bullseye" Detective Stewart reflected on the single gun wound to the victim.

"And the shooter would either have to have known Murray's routine around visiting his office, or it was just an opportune moment. I'm leaning towards the routine theory" Cameron concluded.

"I'll get forensics to check it out in the morning. But I'm not too hopeful about lifting any prints considering our prints are all it"

"And there's something else Cameron. When I returned to my car, my rear tyre had been pierced" Selena added, returning to her seat after topping up Cameron's and her wine glasses.

"Yes, I did notice the temporary spare mini wheel on the back. Thought you must have had a puncture. Hmm that's not good about your tyre being deliberately punctured. Maybe the person doesn't like trespassers or they might have been the killer?"

"No need to put the willies up me anymore than necessary than I'm worried now. I won't sleep tonight" Selena replied dropping her head.

"I don't want you to be scared but you must be mindful Selena. We have a killer on the loose and we don't know if he or she will strike again"

So, you think it might be a woman, Cameron?"

"Anything is possible Selena. Let me ask you this. Who knows the shack exists on the

Barrington- Jones property?" Cameron asked, already ready having his suspects in his mind.

"Obviously Mrs. Barrington – Jones and Brendan" Selena replied.

"Yes, but who else. Somebody current. Who told you there was a hut there in the first place" Cameron said leading Selena to making the only conclusion possible?

"Annie?" a surprised Selena blurted out. "Annie, the conservationist, no way"

"Let's look at it this way. She would have had motive. She would have hated what Barrington-Jones was going to do to the property especially as it would have destroy-yed the koala habit."

Selena stared into space taking in what Cameron had just said. Conservationists are passionate people and they don't come any more passionate than Annie. She would do anything to protect a voiceless animal, especially Australia's national treasure.

"Maybe you have a point, Cameron. Her husband is also part of the Environmental Committee. He'd be right behind her in campaigning to save the koalas. She wears the pants in that family."

"And speaking of the husband, doesn't he own some high-powered rifles? Even you said he was a bit of a marksman" Cameron commented with a glee in his eye, a man on a mission, now in full flight.

Annie and hubby are now firmly in the sights of Detective Stewart's investigation.

CHAPTER 13

Selena slept like a log. The last few days had been exhausting. The thought of Annie being a murderer swirled in her mind causing a delay in her getting off to sleep, but eventually those thoughts passed.

A cool breeze entered through an open window in Selena's bedroom no doubt adding to a peaceful night. Dreams of Cameron extended her slumber until she was woken by a nightmare.

Her father was screaming at her forbidding her marrying Cameron. She woke with a sudden startle only to realize it was just a bad dream.

It was now 7.30 am and Selena quickly jumped out of bed and stumbled her way to the kitchen and filled the coffee pod machine with fresh water.

The Carmichaels walked past the window and waved. "Good morning, Selena. We're just off to town for breakfast. Enjoy your day"

Selena smiled and returned niceties while cursing herself under her breath that she should be a better host and offer her guests breakfast. Bacon and eggs were not her favourite meal and she had not taken an interest in improving her cooking skills. But should she finally snare Detective Stewart she would have to become an expert. Cameron loved his bacon and eggs.

Washing down her toast with the last few sips of her coffee, Selena made her way back to the bedroom, quickly made the bed and then headed to the shower, smiling.

The bed sheets looked kike they had a night of wild thrashing. Perhaps Detective Stewart had played an interesting part in her dreams, but sadly she couldn't remember a thing.

Today was going to be a fun day out. Selena was heading to the northern end of the Gold Coast to do some shopping. She needed a few things for her kitchen and a couple of new wardrobe items might be on the shopping list. Harbour Town Shopping Center had everything Selena could possibly want; all at discount prices.

****

An hour of highway driving, Selena pulled into a parking spot just waiting for her under a shady tree. Selena was always lucky in getting parking spots even at the busiest of times.

The car lot was quite full even though it was just opening time of 10am. Selena entered the northern entry passing the line-up outside the Nike store where budding athletes were anxious to get in and scoop up the latest fashion items.

Active wear was not on Selena's shopping list. She was heading straight to Robin's Kitchen hoping to get some new knives and storage containers. If there was some money left over, a Michael Kors handbag might get a closer inspection.

Robin's Kitchen was having a special one-day sale with an extra 50% off their already reduced prices. Selena looked skyward and acknowledged the man above for her good fortune. She grabbed her carving knives and invested in a new sharpening tool to keep them in perfect working order.

Selena examined the storage containers, testing their lid seals for tightness. Even though she had been a big fan of the Tupperware brand thanks to her Auntie back in India, Selena had found some amazing containers here, now at a bargain price.

There was no way Selena was going to bypass Michael Kors. The hand bag in the window caught her eye as she pushed opened the door; the cool air conditioning making her feel even more welcomed.

The shop was busy. Gold Coast women in their miniskirts, fake tan and boobs, seemed to be at every vantage point. If that wasn't enough, one would let out a screech to the sales attendant "How much is this love?"

Selena would smile as the price tag was clearly evident on each bag; you just had to divide it by two to get today's price. But there again not all girls would have been educated at St. Hilda's.

"Can I help you my dear?" a well-groomed, early fifties attendant asked Selena.

"The bag in the window at the entrance, do you have that in a light tan?"

"Very tasteful Miss. I think I have one out the back. Please take a seat. I just have to finish with the lady at the counter and then I'll get it for you" the sales assistant replied giving Selena the nod of approval.

Within five minutes the assistant was showing Selena the desired bag. The leather was soft and draping it over her shoulder it sung of pure class. The assistant compliment Selena on how well she wore the bag and how it added to her jeans and tan boots.

"How much is this bag?" Selena asked.

"Normally it's over $1000 in our retail stores. Here it's $650. But today you can dazzle your husband with it for just $325"

Selena's eyes met the sales assistant's eyes. This woman was smooth in a genuine way. She certainly knew how to compliment a girl even if she was buying just for herself.

"I'll take it" Selena said pulling her purse from her bag.

"Oh dear, I think your Mimco has seen better days. It should never be seen coming out of your new bag. Mr. Kors would be very disappointed. Come with me. I have something you should look at.

Selena landed at the purse stand and was dutifully shown a couple of styles. The Gold Coast ladies snarled their disapproval as to why Selena was getting so much attention.

"I think this one would be perfect. It matches your new bag like Bacall and Bogart. They are simply made for each other"

"And how much is the purse?" Selena asked.

"Normally $220, but today it's just $110. Tell you what. If you take the pair, the reduced price comes in at $435. I'll do them both for $400?"

Looking at the sales assistant's name badge, Selena commented "Carmen you are very passionate about your products. You are a great ambassador for the brand and even a better sales person. I'll take them both"

Time at flittered away. A spot of lunch was on the cards, and Selena knew a great place nearby. The Intercontinental Hotel at Sanctuary Cove.

The driveway into the Resort was impressive with royal palms bounding both sides of the brick paved road. The hotel was an impressive sight up the man-made hill. In fact, the whole resort was the dream of a 'white-shoed' entrepreneur back in the late eighties.

Today it is the playground of the rich and famous or those who wanted to fake their wealth. The pretenders parked their old clunkers in the public car park and walked up the driveway to the hotel.

Selena felt very comfortable that her 250 SLK Mercedes Benz would be very welcome under the porte-cochere. The car park attendant greeted Selena and offered to valet park her car. Why not she thought as she gave him her details.

Looking back at the entrance she noticed Tommy Llewellyn and Susan Delahunty leaving the hotel and packing some luggage into the book of their vehicle with the odd conservation sticker adorned. Was this the vehicle that had left hurriedly from Barrington-Jones farm the day her tyre was pierced?

Selena hung her head as the couple drove past before commenting "Looks like you guys allow anybody to park here?"

"Oh, that's Tommy Llewellyn. He's here a lot lately Mr. Llewellyn is doing some photography around the Resort with our GM. Plenty of nice things to photograph here" the attendant replied giving Selena an admiring all over glance. Snatching the ticket, Selena headed to the restaurant.

Selena settled for the seafood buffet and took up a table next to the window with the most panoramic view of the fountain and the man-made sandy beach pool. It was a glorious day. Not a cloud in sight and the blue sky was intoxicating.

But Selena was not completely at peace. She kept ruminating about Susan and Tommy. Could they really be responsible for damaging her car?

CHAPTER 14

Selena joined the Gold Coast highway and headed south towards Pottsville while being serenaded by 'Old Blue Eyes'. Frank Sinatra was flown in to open the Sanctuary Cove Resort in 1988 and Selena thought it was only appropriate to farewell the place with a few tunes from Frank.

She dialed Cameron using Siri and invited him over for an early supper. She wanted to bounce her sighting off to him plus show off her new purchases.

Cameron arrived at Selena's place not a minute after five. He would never be late for a free meal especially when Selena had suggested butter chicken was on the menu, his favourite. Hudson was in toe, his nose investigating the mouthwatering aroma coming from the kitchen. Unfortunately for Hudson that would be as close to Indian food he would come tonight.

Selena paraded her purchases in front of Cameron with a spark of approval. He was firmly fixated on his meal. Hudson seemed to be more appreciative and let out a couple of woofs. They worked and soon Cameron responded with compliments that clearly showed he was no fashionista.

Selena wondered if she would ever train Cameron to be more interested in her appearance. She couldn't put it down to being the Australian way, Indian men were just the same. Perhaps she needed to reserve her showing to her female friends.

"You'll never guess who I saw at Sanctuary Cove today" Selena said hoping to get Cameron's attention.

"No, who? Cameron replied with taking his eyes of his swirling fork carefully combining the butter chicken and basmati rice. He guided the food into his mouth savoring it as it entered, his eyes almost glazing over. Finally, he looked at Selena. Hudson woofed again; this time approving of his master paying attention to Selena.

"Susan Delahunty and Tommy Llewellyn"

"Really? I wonder what they were doing there?" Cameron replied intuitively

"Mr. Llewellyn is doing some photography for the hotel apparently "Selena replied.

Cameron pondered on Selena's update adding Susan and Tommy to the growing list of suspects. Unfortunately, Murray Barrington-

Jones had ticked a lot of people off over his lifetime. At this rate, just about everybody in town would be on it.

What Cameron needed was a process of elimination. He excused himself from the dining table, thanked Selena for a fabulous dinner and headed to the verandah.

"I just want to go through my list of suspects; see if I can cross anybody off" Detective Stewart advised Selena moving outside with pen and paper in hand.

"Sure. I'll grab us some dessert and pop out to give you a hand"

Apple pie and custard complimented a great dinner even if the custard was bought. To Selena's way of thinking, you have to acknowledge your weaknesses in the kitchen. Her custard always turned out lumpy and while Cameron smiled in the early days, she knew he preferred Jacaranda Custard.

No use tormenting the poor man even though watching him almost choke with every mouthful seemed entertaining, it was not going to win his heart. Her mother would say to *win a man's heart, is through his stomach*. Another pearl of wisdom Selena fondly remembers about her mother. The only thing she questioned though was how much food a man needed. Cameron Stewart seemed to need a buffet.

"Who's at the top of your list Detective" Selena smiled as she took up her seat opposite.

Stewart had already carved out a few names based on who he perceived had the strongest motive.

Susan Delahunty was at the top even though she didn't know the contents of the will. She stood to benefit by getting the property which in turn would give comfort to Brendan. A mother would do anything to protect her child, maybe even murder.

"What about Annie Greer?" Selena asked.

She was in the mix for sure. A conservationist with a passion to save koalas. The Barrington-Jones farm was home to a koala habitat and Murray was about to wipe them out. Annie would have hated that. Paul Greer was a gun owner and crack shooter. They'd make a formidable pair in protecting the environment at any cost.

"She's right up there along with Brian Brady from the van park" Cameron replied chewing on his pencil. The case wouldn't be solved tonight

Cameron decided to call it a night. He thanked Selena for her hospitality, pecked her on the cheek and made his way to his car.

Selena sighed as she gathered up the plates in readiness for the dishwasher. Sometimes she wished Detective Stewart could take a night off 'detecting' and focus on her. It would be even nicer if he stayed the night, but they are still away off that happening. Maybe it's a police thing to always be on duty. She stopped for a moment and pondered. *Could she be a policeman's wife if all he did was work?*

Selena decided to take advantage of her free time. Even though she had a big time, she wasn't tired. Discussions around the Barrington-Jones murder had kept her brain cells active, so why not use this energy for her benefit.

Selena sat at her office desk, her father's originally. Solid timber with leather inserts, it had a commanding presence in the room. Selena felt like the President of the United States, the Commander in Chief, making decisions in her own Oval Office.

Rousi Sharma had finalized many a business deal at this desk. Indentations, knicks and inscriptions made it his and reminded Selena of all the good things her dad had done for the family.

Selena pulled up her future bookings on her laptop. The next few weeks would be busy with the cottage 80% occupied. Guests come to relax, read, take in the region's birdlife and soak up the village atmosphere of Pottsville and the Tweed Valley.

They also came for Selena's cooking either as students or devourers. I any case Selena decided she should do a little preparation.

She returned to the kitchen and started preparing a vegetable dahl and a beef madras. Normally she would shy away from spicy food as Westerners preferred mild food over a fire burning madras curry. But with a guest named Singh coming to stay she decided more spice might be to his liking.

With the curries simmering away, Selena made herself some tea and headed out to the verandah. The moon shone brightly lighting up the night sky and the cool breeze refreshed Selena from her warm kitchen.

She thought more about Cameron's list. Could Susan really have kill her ex-husband? She thought about Cameron's comments about a mother's scorn. Not being a mother herself, Selena found it difficult to feel the anger of a mother, but agreed it could be possible.

Returning to the stove Selena turned the flame to very low. These dishes would simmer all night making them tender for her incoming guests.

Tomorrow she would take a drive into town to catch up with Susan Delahunty.

CHAPTER 15

Selena knocked on the door of Susan's rented house. She probably could have stayed at the house but the place gave her the creeps. Besides being a crime scene for a while, she didn't want to be reminded of Murray every corner she turned.

"Hi Selena. Nice to see you. Something smells nice. You had better come in" Susan announced stepping aside to let Selena pass. "What have to got here? WOW hummingbird cake. Take up a comfy seat in the lounge and I'll put the kettle on"

The house was pleasant but modest, set one street back off Coronation Street. Two storied, Susan occupied the lower level with its own kitchenette and bathroom facilities. The outlook to the lush green grass was very calming, something Ms. Delahunty would no doubt appreciate after this tumultuous time.

The owners of the property finished the property with some exquisite, personal touches. The Royal Doulton tea set including cake stand did not go amiss with Selena.

"Love the snow dome Susan. Is that your personal touch?" Selena asked reading the Sanctuary Cove inscription.

"Oh yes, it is; a bit of fun. I've just got back from the Coast. My sister lives there and we caught up for lunch at George's Paragon Seafood restaurant. She bought me the dome, her sense of humour I guess"

Selena sipped her tea and knowing full well she had seen Susan and Tommy at the Intercontinental, she asks "And did you stay for a couple of days with your sister?"

"Yes, it was nice to catch up" Susan replied. Selena didn't buy it though.

"How are you feeling in yourself? It must have come as quite a shock for you about Murray?"

"Yes, it was even though we had been estranged for a while. He had his faults Selena but nobody should be murdered.

"And I guess you were just getting over the news that he had started divorce proceedings against you"

Susan dropped her head, her eyes filling with emotion. She drank her tea and composed herself.

"It was very hard. Murray was my first love. I know there were rumours about me and Tommy Llewellyn, but that is all they were, rumours." Tommy was not a rumour in Selena's eyes; she saw them at the hotel on the weekend.

"He's a photographer?" Selena asked.

"Mr. Paparazzi he was called. He's the photographer you call in for that special moment. He worked in London for decades around the Princess Di era. He was pretty dashing in tails and a top hat at some of those Royal Garden parties. Quite a ladies' man I would think.

Personal friend of Mick from the Stones and he even attended Rod Stewart's third wedding. He was the photographer's photographer"

Selena thought he must be still doing ok to spring for a couple of three-hundred-dollar nights at the Intercontinental "You say was?"

"The work is just not here. He's photographed a few Instagram influencers in Byron but they a few and far between. Today everybody is going digital and with touch up companies online offering mood lighting and younger looking skin"

"So do you guys still catch up?" Selena asked.

"No, every now and then but not often" Susan replied with a smile as if butter wouldn't melt in her mouth. "Of course, he contacted me when he heard of Murray's passing. He even offered me some money towards Murray's funeral?"

"That's kind of him" Selena replied thinking the two must have been close at some stage for Tommy to offer money. Maybe still close according to the hotel visit.

"How do you feel about Brendan getting the property?"

" It would be his one day, why not sooner. I'll be fine and if I need a hand, I'm sure Brendan will look after me. He's a good boy like that" Susan replied with a content look.

Selena wished Susan well and headed to the door. "My guests are expecting dinner tonight, so I need to make tracks"

Susan opened the door and the pair were met by a tall male figure, blocking the exit although not intentionally.

"Tommy, what a nice surprise. Selena, I don't think you've met Tommy Llewellyn before, have you?"

Selena stretched out her hand and exchanged pleasantries with Tommy. While they hadn't personally met, Selena felt their paths had crossed. But looking at Tommy's car, she was certain.

"Save the koalas" sticker was the same one that she saw in the distance leaving the Barrington Jones property the day her tyre was slashed.

Selena and Tommy exchanged pleasantries while she bid Susan a good day.

Selena opened her driver's door and Hudson quickly sat up to assume the guard position, giving her a 'welcome back look.

"That was interesting Hudson. Susan seems not that fussed about Brendan getting the house even though it'll make her life a little more difficult. I suppose that's what parents want for their children; the best.

Hudson sat with his head cocked, his eyes fixed on Selena as if he was taking it all in. Selena returned a comforting smile; Hudson was her child.

Selena drove into her driveway passing her guests who had been out for a leisurely stroll. "Morning, a great day for it" Selena commented as passed them and waving from the car.

Cameron Stewart wasn't far behind her. A quick coffee and croissant were on his mind before he headed into the station.

"Any closer to solving the case Detective?" Selena liked to throw in a bit of formality every now and then just to keep things real. In some ways it was also Selena protecting herself in case things didn't develop with Detective Stewart.

"Unfortunately, not. I'm a bit baffled on this one" Cameron replied dunking his croissant into his coffee. Selena squirmed at the sight but recalled *it's the French way*, even though Cameron was as Aussie as they come.

Selena let Cameron know that she had been with Susan having a cup of tea and offering her support. Cameron wasn't convinced about the support line. More like snooping he thought.

"Susan mentioned she was a little worried about being left out of the will but glad at the same time that Brendan was to be looked after. Tommy was giving her advice"

"Oh yeah what sort of advice would that be. You know he's in a bit of financial trouble? Apparently, he owes a few big magazines work he took big advances against and never delivered upon. And not to mention a few wedding couples who never go their photos even though they had paid in advance. Our Mr. Llewellyn is a bit dodgy" Cameron explained.

" Hmm, that makes sense. Apparently, he is suggesting to Susan that Brendan should continue the build of the Oasis Resort and that he could oversee the operation for her"

"Sounds like he's trying to get his grubby mitts on Brendan's money to me"

Selena also let Cameron know that Tommy's car had a bumper sticker 'Save the Koalas' on it referencing it the one that she possibly saw leaving Murray's property; the day her tyre was slashed.

"Do you still have the note that was left on your car that day?" Cameron asked. I might get our Mr. Llewellyn to write out an invoice for me and see if we have a match?"

CHAPTER 16

Selena kept up her investigation on Tommy. She googled his name and checked out his Facebook profile.

Not surprisingly both weren't that favourable. His business website was dogged with poor reviews, many one and two stars from disgruntled customers. Facebook revealed he didn't have many friends except one interesting contact, probably more so than a friend.

Elizabeth Llewellyn, Tommy's ex-wife, a real estate agent in Cabarita Beach, was just one of his thirty-seven friends.

Selena found Elizabeth's mobile and quickly gave her a call.

"Elizabeth, this is Selena Sharma. I'm wondering if you'd be in today. I'd like to pop in for a chat. I'm thinking of getting a unit near the beach" An appointment for midafternoon was arranged.

Cabarita Beach was just a quick fifteen-minute drive from Pottsville. Both towns exuded a laid-back ambience although Cabarita was more popular with the local surfers.

Llewellyn Properties had a prominent position on Tweed Coast Road and was conveniently located opposite the Beach Hotel and surf club. Elizabeth Llewellyn frequented both establishments regularly supposedly in the name of securing business, although the locals would testify on a stack of bibles that Elizabeth was partial to a wine or two most afternoons from 3pm.

Selena arrived early and decided to forgo coffee in the nearby café and immediately entered the real estate agency.

She was greeted by a sixty something, blond bleached hair, sun baked woman busily talking on the phone with her left hand raised indicating to Selena not to interrupt her as she was on an important call.

Selena gave a cool, half smile and looked around the shop, picking up a couple of brochures and viewing the odd property listing in the window. The shop was small with three desks, presumably for other sales people. At the rear of the was an enclosed office which Selena guessed must be Elizabeth's office. It looked empty though.

The lady at the reception counter continued on her call as if Selena was invisible, occasionally looking up, testing how much more time she had to chat. Selena pocketed a couple of business cards to help pass the time.

"I better go love. I've just had somebody pop in" the receptionist finally ending her call.

"Hi I'm Judy. How can I help you?"

Judy was definitely on the wrong side of sixty. Bleached blonde hair with dark roots protruding, wrinkles like mountain cravats which indicated a life in the sun and that no amount of Botox would ever fix. Hot pink acrylic nails most likely from the Asian nail bar down the street beamed to all and sundry. Absolutely gordy.

"I have an appointment with Elizabeth Lewellyn at 3 pm. My name is Selena Sharma" Selena explained. She could see the cogs turning in Judy's mind ever so slowly.

"She's not in love. She's been held up at another appointment. Are you the lady that runs the cooking school in Pottsville" Judy enquired?

"I do love a good butter chicken, but only if it's mild" Judy added trying to impress Selena with her knowledge of Indian cuisine.

Selena smiled and started to wonder if her trip to Cabarita was going to be a total waste of time.

"That's a pity. I wanted to get some information on beachfront units" Selena mentioned keeping the conversation moving "and I was hoping Elizabeth could fill me in"

"I'll get you a couple of brochures love" Judy replied as she headed towards the back of the office to a bookshelf, grabbing a few brochures that would hopefully satisfy Selena.

"No other sales people in either today?" Selena asked.

We only have Mark now with us. He's part of the furniture really but he's at his other office; the bowls club"

"Tell me Judy, is Elizabeth any relation to Tommy Llewellyn the photographer in Pottsville?"

"Her ex, love. Gosh they've been divorced for yonks. And a good thing too" Judy commented in a tone that proudly defended her boss.

Selena's facial inquisitiveness prompted Judy to expand.

"This business might not look much but Elizabeth does ok. In fact, she's always done ok; good in fact. And Tommy always had his hand in the till. A sponge.

When he was in the business, he was supposed to photograph the houses for sale but he often messed up. Late delivery or photos not done at all. We had clients screaming at us and Elizabeth started to lose a lot of business.

But Tommy didn't seem to care. He was a man living way above his station. A bit of a dreamer really and lazy to boot.

Elizabeth got sick of him with his hand in the till. She finally kicked the parasite out. Best thing she ever did"

Selena took in the commentary of Judy, confirming her suspicions about Mr. Llewellyn. Tommy had a history of poor financial decisions and his problems haven't gone away today. But is that enough to kill a man?

CHAPTER 17

Detective Stewart arrived at Selena's guesthouse around morning tea time clutching a sponge roll in his right hand and delicately placed it on the side board, beaming at Selena as he did it.

"Cameron that looks nice but you know I don't eat cakes laden with cream. You bought that for yourself I suspect. Let me put the kettle on"

Cameron took up his usual seat at the wooden farmhouse table in the kitchen rubbing his hand across the grain. The table could tell many stories and Cameron was eager to tell another.

"I had a call with Brendan earlier this morning. At first, he seemed a little hesitant but then he passed on a nice compliment to me.

Apparently, his dad Murray, had a lot of time for me, which I was a bit surprised about considering Mr. Barrington-Jones was a bit dodgy living on the other side of the law."

"That's nice Cameron" Selena replied pouring his tea and sliding a think slice of sponge cake across the table. "Let me get you a cake fork. Do go on"

"He was with his mother the other morning when the solicitor phoned to say that the insurance policy on Murray was ready for payment. He was surprised how quick it was but grateful for his new found nest egg.

Anyway, Tommy had shown up that morning as well. Brendan never got along with him. He thought he was using his mother but

142

understood why his father wanted to divorce his mother. Murray had explained that Susan was having an affair with Tommy and that simply was the end of the marriage.

Brendan was in his room when he felt like a snack and made his way to the kitchen to make a sandwich. He overheard Tommy chatting to his mother about the insurance payout and how he could help her with her $1.5 million share. He insisted he should accompany her to the bank with the cheque."

"And as we know Cameron, Tommy is in a bit of financial hot water. I've heard in excess of $1 million"

"How do you know that, Selena?" Cameron asked

Selena shrugged off the question with a vacant look, hoping Cameron would not push for more details. Selena thew a curve ball trying to take Cameron off the scent.

"Have you ever considered Brendan as a suspect in his father's murder?" Selena asked pushing another slice of cake across the table towards Cameron.

"Absolutely. Everybody is a suspect but I eliminated him after I spoke to his college room monitor who vouched that Brenden was in residence on the day of his father's killing"

"All day?" Selena questioned. Detective Stewart was not 100% satisfied now.

"So, we need to begin a process of elimination to narrow down the killer then" Selena commented knowing full well she was poking the bear; and he bit.

"I need to eliminate the suspects Selena, not we" Cameron replied in a firm tone.

"Of course, Detective, that's what I meant. What are your thoughts on Annie?"

"She's been placed at a talk far away from here at the time of Murray's death. And I can't see her using a gun to kill Murray or anything else for that matter. It goes against her conservationist way, I would think." Cameron elaborated.

"But her husband has a rifle, is a member of a gun club and is a pretty good shot I hear" Selena commented.

"True he's not fully in the clear but I can't see a connection with Murray and him. There would be nothing for him to gain, except the stopping of the golf club development which Annie would love."

Selena smiled and replied "Some men will do anything to win the hearts of their women? The subtle comment washed straight over Cameron's head.

"What about Brian and the crew at Blue Hills caravan park? They definitely had a grudge against Murray. Look where they are now thanks to Murray?"

"Yes, their shit existence would play heavily on their minds. Even though they would never be able to forgive Murray and it would be a strong reason to kill him, I couldn't see Brian shooting Murray. He'd worry about not seeing his son and that would way heavily on his heart"

"Well, I guess we are left with Susan and Tommy. Both with financial motives. Even though Susan didn't know she was being cut out of the will, her prospects for a comfortable life away from Murray was limited. Having to rely on the pension and handouts from family and friends is not a great position to be in"

"I guess not" Cameron replied continuing on with "and we know Tommy's photography business is bleeding cash. When he was having the affair with Susan, he probably though he was on a good wicket. But when Murray enforced the pre-nup, Susan got nothing in the divorce settlement. Maybe Tommy needed to devise another plan?"

CHAPTER 18

By the process of elimination, Tommy became the number one suspect. Could he be that cold to rekindle and old relationship with Susan with the intention of marrying her to get his hands on half of the property?

Selena with her romantic heart couldn't entertain such a calculated thought. Surely humans couldn't be that manipulative. Tommy and Susan were old flames way before Murray came on the scene. It's not uncommon for that flame never to be extinguished.

Cameron wasn't so convinced. Maybe it was a male thing. Maybe he wasn't overwhelmed with romantic thoughts that could blind his detective deductibility skills. Selena had her views on this as well.

For Detective Stewart, Tommy was always skating on thin ice when it came to money. He could see an end to his problems if he could just get Susan to leave Murray and marry him. But he got impatient. He let it be known around town that he was rekindling his passion with Susan.

When Murray filed for divorce, Tommy thought he was a step closer with his plan. He put in play to divorce Elizabeth, a successful real estate agent and pursue Susan.

But he never knew of the pre-nup between Murray and Susan. His dirty greedy plan to get his hands on about three million dollars of real estate, had backfired. Elizabeth was glad to be rid of the parasite, and there was no taking him back. Tommy was snookered.

"The only thing that puzzles me" Cameron started "is that Susan only found out she was cut out of the will after Murray was killed"

"So that's when Brendan became an important person to Tommy" Selena surmised.

The pair had been tossing the case around for hours. They seemed to be going around in circles when Selena suggested a break. Cameron nodded. His head felt like it was splitting.

"How about I refuel those brain cells of yours Detective with a special butter chicken, fluffy basmati rice and a freshly made naan bread" Selena said in a tempting voice. Selena could cook an array of curry dishes but butter chicken was Detective Stewart's favourite.

An hour later, Detective Stewart was scrapping the last of the butter chicken sauce off his plate with the last piece of naan bread. "That was superb, Selena" The best you've ever cooked"

"No dessert Detective, but I do have a couple of salted caramel Connoisseur ice creams in the fridge?"

"I think one of those has my name written all over it" Cameron replied.

Cameron's mobile phone rang out from the lounge room, vibrating across the coffee table.

"Detective Stewart here"

Cameron listened intently. "Ok Susan, keep calm. Light your place up like a Christmas tree. Turn all the lights on. Lock the back door and windows. I'm on my way"

"What's going on Cameron" Selena stated inquisitively while gathering her car keys.

"You stay here Selena. I can handle this. Susan is expecting a visitor"

CHAPTER 19

Detective Stewart high tailed it to the Barrington-Jones property constantly praying to himself that he would not be late. Surely Mr. Rudinski would not have disobeyed Stewart's orders to stay away from Susan?

Tommy's car was parked out front. The house felt cold as he scrambled up the front stairs. Only the light in the lounge was visible.

He barged through the front door to be met by a trembling Susan, her jaw uncontrollably shaking and tears streaming down her face.

Behind her was an overweight, pasty, unshaven image, feet slightly apart firmly anchoring himself to the floor and menacingly pointing a rifle at both of them.

Detective Stewart entered the room with his hands in the air. The gunman took three steps back. It was Brian Brady from the Blue Hills Caravan Park.

Stewart glanced to his left. Brendan was seated on the couch looking reasonably calm. Behind Brian lay Tommy Llewellyn in a pool of blood, a single rifle shot wound to his head.

Brian motioned Susan and Detective Stewart into the lounge room.

But before anybody moved, Brian let out an almighty scream, enough of a distraction for Stewart to lunge at him and wrestle the rifle away. Susan ran to Brendan on the couch embracing him with a teary, long hug.

Firmly pinning Brian to the floor, he discovered why Brian had let out an almighty scream. Hudson had locked his jaws onto Brian's calf and was not letting go. Selena stood at the back door near the kitchen. For once Detective Stewart was glad Selena had disobeyed his request to stay put.

"Brian Brady, I am charging you with the fatal shooting of Tommy Llewellyn. And if my suspicions are correct this is also the rifle that killed Murray Barrington–Jones. You have…"

"Hang on Detective. I've not shot or killed anybody" Brian butted in protesting his innocence.

Detective Stewart directed Brian to the couch, sitting him next to Brendan.

"When I arrived here, I found Tommy lying on the floor dead. I picked up the rifle and pointed it at these two. Then you came bursting in"

"Finger prints on the rifle will determine who's been handling it. So, you're saying there's more than yours Brian?" What are you doing here anyway?" Stewart asked.

"I received a call from an anonymous male to be here tonight. He said he'd fix me up. I took that to mean that I'd get my money back from the shenanigans Barrington–Jones pulled over me and others years ago costing us everything we had. Was it Tommy that called you?" Stewart asked.

"Don't know. I can't remember the last time we ever spoke" Brian replied.

"What's your side of the story?" Selena asked, hoping a softer woman's voice might widen the conversation.

"Tommy was dead when I arrived" a shaking, sobbing Susan replied. I had received a call earlier from him saying he wanted to meet me at the farm. That's when I called Detective Stewart. I was nervous"

"And what were your movements, Brendan?" Detective Stewart asked.

"I got here not long after Mum arrived". Tommy was dead and Brian was kneeling over him"

"Were you aware Tommy was having money problems Susan?" Susan nodded. Is it possible he lured you up here with the intention of firstly marrying you, then later killing you to claim his stake on your money?

"No that's absurd. He loved me. And I loved him. I had never stopped loving him, even when I was married to Murray" Susan broke down. Brendan grunted a noise of disapproval, gritting his teeth and glaring at his mother.

Brendan's demeanor didn't go unnoticed on Detective Stewart.

"What's up son? Why are you so angry?" Susan asked Brendan. "Actually, come to think of it, how did you end up here? I never called you"

"Shut up Mum. You stupid cow! You've always been used by men. Firstly, by Dad, then that loser Tommy. No wonder Dad wanted to divorce you. He was the laughing stock of town. His wife having an affair with Pottsville's playboy.

People would snigger behind his back. He couldn't go out as he might be the butt of somebody's joke.

And you were one of those weak story spreading pricks weren't you, Brian.

It was me who rang you from the pay phone on Coronation Avenue. Once I baited you with the possibility of getting your money back, you dived in hook, line and sinker. I bet you burnt rubber from that hole of a

157

caravan park to the farm; you weak pathetic overweight loser.

Dad never conned you out of the money with a false soil report. It was your casualness and mere stupidity that cost you and all your friends their money. You and only you Brian"

Brian looked at Brendan gob smacked.

"And I suppose Tommy Llewellyn had to be stopped marrying your mother, Brendan?" Detective Stewart asked.

"Captain Casual was our Tommy" Brendan smirked. He thought Mum was getting all of Dad's money. His business was sinking. He needed cash fast. Elizabeth was sick of all his affairs. She wasn't bailing him out of any more problems.

But he never checked the fine print. I was the recipient of Dad's estate. Then I learned he was planning on killing Mum in order to get the cash. It was him that killed Dad. Annie, the old environmentalist duck told me that Tommy was a crack marksman when I was on one of her tree hugging adventures one day.

I could have told you that Detective Stewart, but revenge would taste so much sweeter. So close, yet so far.

Susan began sobbing uncontrollably. Her boy would be going to jail for the killing of Tommy Llewellyn.

Detective Stewart ushered the local Lismore police into the lounge who immediately arrested Brendan Barrington–Jones. Brian remained with some other officers and answered their questions, clearing his name of any wrong doing.

"Are you going to thank Hudson for saving your life Detective Stewart?" Selena asked with inquisitive eyes?

Cameron Stewart smiled and a look of thankfulness covered his face. Hudson knew a juicy steak was waiting for him at home.

ABOUT THE AUTHOR

C T Mitchell is an Amazon bestselling author of 40+ mystery short reads and novels with a thriller edge. He is multiple 5-star recipient in the 2017 Readers Choice Awards for his novel Murder Secret (formerly published as Breaking Point) and is currently shortlisted to turn this book into film with negotiations occurring with Amazon Prime and Netflix.

Street educated; Australian-born C T Mitchell has traveled the world in his business dealings as a real estate negotiator encountering many interesting characters; some outright crooks. He brings these experiences as well as a love for mystery thrillers to his writing.

His fast-paced Detective Jack Creek Mysteries weave together traditional police procedural practice, global locations, and a hint of thrillers. Described by readers as "Rebus in a Valentino suit" Jack Creed is the 'hard copper' you want on your case.

Dead Shot #1
Dead Ringer #2
Dead Wrong #3
Dead Boss #4
Dead Stakes #5
Dead Lucky #6
Dead Silence #7

Murder Secret (short listed – Book to Film)

C T Mitchell also writes cozy mysteries.

Lady Elizabeth Turnbull, the 50 something, widow, is the bane of Detective Tom Sullivan's life, but usually solves his cases. He's secretly appreciative.

Murder at the Fete #1
Murder in the Village #2
Murder in the Cemetery #3
Murder in the Valley #4
Murder at the Manor #5
Murder Shot #6

Three more cozy mystery series featuring Kate Mackenzie's Sugar N Spice Cupcake Company, Father Douglas and Selena Sharma Mysteries are also on Amazon.

C T Mitchell splits his time in both Brisbane and Cabarita Beach - a sleepy seaside village in northern NSW, Australia - the home of his award-winning books. To grab two free mystery bestsellers, please visit www.CTMitchellBooks.com , or follow him on Facebook or Twitter.

FREE DOWNLOADS

Grab to free downloads of C T Mitchell's
Amazon bestsellers here
https://FreeCrimeBooks.com